First published 2000 in *The Macmillan Treasury of Nursery Stories*
This collection first published 2010 by Macmillan Children's Books
a division of Macmillan Publishers Limited
20 New Wharf Road, London N1 9RR
Basingstoke and Oxford
Associated companies throughout the world
www.panmacmillan.com

ISBN: 978-0-230-74996-2

A CIP catalogue record for this book is available from the British Library.

Printed in China

MACMILLAN CHILDREN'S BOOKS

Hansel and Gretel
and other stories

Retold by
Mary Hoffman

Illustrated by
Anna Currey

Hansel and Gretel

Once upon a time a poor woodcutter and his second wife lived on the edge of a forest. The woodcutter's son, Hansel, and his daughter, Gretel, by his first wife, lived with them. They were very poor indeed and there came a day when they had no more food and no more money to buy any more food.

"Whatever are we to do, husband?" said the wife. "We cannot feed our children and we are all going to starve."

"I don't know," replied the wretched man. "I suppose we must keep on cutting wood and hope that things will get better."

"That's no good," said the wife. "We need a plan. I think we should take the children out into the forest with us, give them a last slice of bread each and then contrive to leave them, so that they are lost."

"But they will be devoured by wild beasts!" the woodcutter protested.

"Better that than for us to have to watch them starve. It will be a quicker death," said his wife.

And in the end, reluctantly, the woodcutter agreed with her. Now Hansel, who was a light sleeper, had heard all this conversation and went to tell his sister. She was horrified. "What can we do?" she cried.

"Don't worry, sister," said Hansel. "They may have a plan, but so do I."

And he went out into the moonlight and picked up handfuls of white pebbles from outside their hut.

In the morning, the whole family set off for the forest but, as they walked, Hansel kept stopping to leave a trail of white pebbles so that he and Gretel could find their way back. When his stepmother noticed that he was not keeping up, she asked

what he was doing and he replied, "I'm looking back because I can see my little white cat sitting on the roof as if to say goodbye to me."

"Foolish boy!" said his stepmother. "That is not your little white cat. It is the sunlight shining on the roof tiles."

The parents left their children, with a slice of bread each and a warm fire, in a glade in the forest, while they worked at cutting trees. But the woodcutter had fixed up a broken branch so that it knocked against a withered tree in the wind and sounded like his axe. By the time the children had discovered the trick, their parents were long gone.

But they ate their bread and waited till nightfall, when the moon came out. Then they followed the trail of white

pebbles back to their home. When they knocked at the door, their stepmother scolded them for getting lost, but their father was very pleased to see them.

And it happened that the food shortage eased and so the father was very glad that the plan to lose them in the forest had not succeeded. Time passed and there was another famine in the land. Again the woodcutter's family was reduced to their last half-loaf of bread and with no prospect of any more food.

So the woodcutter's wife suggested the same idea again. "Only this time we must take them further into the forest so that they cannot find their way back. This is the only way to save ourselves."

Secretly the woodcutter thought it would be better to share their last mouthfuls of food with their children and all starve together. But since he had said yes the time before, he didn't know how to say no this time, so in the end he agreed. But the children had overheard their parents talking and knew what was going to happen. Only this time the door was locked and Hansel could not collect any pebbles. "Don't worry," he told his sister. "I shall think of something."

In the morning, the parents gave each child a slice of bread, but Hansel crumbled his in his pocket and dropped the crumbs behind him as they walked. "What are you doing?" asked his stepmother sharply.

"I am looking at my little white pigeon on the roof that looks as if it is saying goodbye to me," said Hansel.

"Nonsense!" said his stepmother. "That is no pigeon. It is the morning sunlight shining on the chimney."

The parents took their children deeper into the forest than before and built them a fire. Then they went away to work, telling the children they would be back before dark. Of course, they never returned. At midday, Gretel shared her piece of bread with Hansel. And when it got dark and the moon came up, they tried to find their way home, but birds had come and eaten up all Hansel's crumbs, so they had no trail to follow.

"Now we are truly lost," wept Gretel.

"No, no," said Hansel, trying to keep her spirits up. "We'll soon find the way."

But they didn't. They walked all that night and all the next day, lying down to sleep in the leaves when they were tired, but they were still no nearer to finding their home.

By now they were very hungry, for there was nothing but a few berries to eat in the forest. They were lucky that they hadn't come across any wild beasts, because they would have been tasty morsels for a hungry bear or wolf.

Tired and hungry, they eventually stumbled into a clearing where there was a cosy little house. And when they got nearer to it, they could see that it was all made of food! The roof was made of gingerbread, the windows of spun sugar and the door and window sills of lovely sweet cake.

It was a long time since Hansel and Gretel had tasted anything sweet and they were very hungry, so they couldn't resist. Hansel reached up and broke off a piece of gingerbread roof. And Gretel, I'm sorry to say, began to lick one of the windows. How delicious it tasted!

But then the cottage door flew open and a very old woman came hobbling out on two sticks. The children were terrified but she seemed kindly enough.

"What charming children!" she said. "Who brought you here?"

Hansel and Gretel explained how they were lost in the forest and the old woman invited them in and gave them apple pancakes and glasses of milk. She didn't say anything about finding them eating her house.

When their stomachs were full, the children became

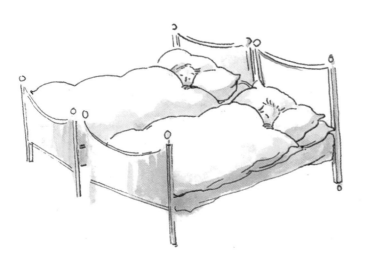

very sleepy and the old woman showed them to two little white beds. Hansel and Gretel thought themselves in heaven as they fell asleep. But they were wrong.

The old woman wasn't really sweet and kind. She was really a witch! She had it in mind to eat the two children and, in fact, her house was made of sweet goodies especially to entice children to her. She was a very wicked witch indeed.

In the morning, before the children were awake, she seized Hansel and locked him in a cage, because he was the plumper of the two. Then she shook Gretel awake and told her she must do all the housework and cook nice food for her brother, who was to be fattened up to be eaten.

Gretel was horrified, but she had to do what the witch told her. Now Hansel was fed chicken stew and sausages and gravy and dumplings and spotted dick with custard, while Gretel got only dry crackers and cheese rinds. Every day the witch reached into the cage to feel Hansel's finger, but her eyesight was so bad that he was able to deceive her by thrusting a chicken bone out.

"Why does he never get

any fatter?" grumbled the witch, as she felt the bone.

But after four weeks she was too impatient to wait any more.

"Boil up water on the stove," she told Gretel. "I'm going to cook that boy today."

Gretel wept and wailed but it was no good. She had to heat up the water.

"I'm going to bake some bread to have with him," said the witch. "I've made the dough. Now just creep into the oven for me and tell me if it's hot enough."

Now the wicked witch meant to shut the oven door on Gretel and bake her! But Gretel had her suspicions so she asked the witch, "What exactly do you mean? Would you mind showing me yourself?"

"Stupid girl!" muttered the witch. But she clambered into the oven and BANG! Gretel shut the door on her. And the wicked witch was burned to a cinder. Gretel rushed to get her keys from the rack and released Hansel from his cage. They embraced each other heartily, crying with relief over their escape from the witch.

Now they had nothing to fear so they explored the house and found chests of pearls and other precious jewels. Hansel stuffed his pockets with them, saying, "These are better than pebbles!" Gretel filled the pockets of her pinafore. She also helped herself to a nice piece of pie and a couple of apples but Hansel felt so full that he wasn't interested in food.

Their next thought was to get home, but they had no idea where they were. They started off in what they thought was the right direction. Before long they came to a broad stretch of water with no bridge in sight. But there was a white duck swimming on the water and Gretel asked her if she would take them across.

When they were both across, they walked a bit further and after a while their surroundings began to seem familiar. Then with joy they recognised the path to their old home. They rushed in through the door and found their father sitting very lonely in the downstairs room.

Their stepmother had died while they had been away and their father had missed his children terribly. He was so glad to see them again. And he was amazed when he saw all the pearls and jewels. From that day onwards they always had enough to eat. But Hansel never touched gingerbread again.

Sleeping Beauty

There was once a king and queen who longed to have a child. They waited many years but, at last, the queen gave birth to a beautiful baby girl. How proud the king was of his little daughter! He wanted her christening party to be the grandest ever seen.

He invited all their friends and relations from far and wide and also invited the fairies who lived in the kingdom. He thought that they might give the little princess special gifts. But there were thirteen fairies in the land and the king had only twelve sets of special gold plates and cups and knives and forks. He had to leave one fairy off his invitation list, so he chose the grumpiest and most unkind.

When the day came, there was a splendid feast and everyone had a very grand place setting, but none so grand as the golden ones set before the twelve fairies. After the feast, the fairies started to give their magic gifts to the princess.

One gave beauty, one kindness, one wealth, one a lovely singing voice and so on, until eleven fairies had bestowed their blessings and the princess was a very lucky baby indeed. But then, disaster! The thirteenth fairy, the

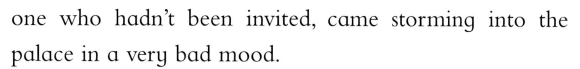

one who hadn't been invited, came storming into the palace in a very bad mood.

"This is my gift," she said. "When the princess is fifteen years old, she will prick her finger and fall down dead!" Then she gathered up her skirts and flounced out without another word.

Everyone was appalled by what had happened, but the twelfth fairy, who hadn't yet given her gift, said, "I cannot completely change the last wish, but I can soften it. She shall not die, but shall sleep for a hundred years, she and the whole court."

After that, the party cheered up, because the princess was not doomed to die after all and fifteen years seemed a long time. All the same, the king issued a decree that all needles, pins and spindles should be banished from the kingdom, which meant that all sewing and spinning had to be done outside its borders, which was very inconvenient.

All the good gifts that the fairies had given the princess at the christening made her life pleasant. She was so lovely to look at that everyone loved her and she had a sweet nature to go with it. She sang like a nightingale, danced like a leaf in the wind and could play several musical

instruments, as well as being able to paint and draw and write elegant verses.

She had a golden childhood but, on her fifteenth birthday, when her parents were busy arranging her party, she went exploring in the palace and came across a staircase she had never seen before. She climbed the winding stairs and came to a little room, where an old woman sat working at a spinning-wheel.

"Good day, mother," said the princess, politely. "What are you doing?" Remember, she had never seen a spinning-wheel, for all spindles were banned from the kingdom.

"Why, I am spinning, child," said the old woman, who was really the bad fairy in disguise.

"And what is that, which spins round so merrily?" asked the princess, and she touched the spindle. Immediately, it pricked her finger and she fell down onto the bed in that room, in a deep sleep.

The king and queen also fell asleep, and so did all the courtiers and servants. The horses went to sleep in their stables, the dogs in the yard, the pigeons on the roof. Even the fire blazing in the grate was frozen in stillness.

And so they all stayed for a hundred years and no one grew any older. But round the castle sprang up a huge hedge of rose-bushes with long thorns, so dense and tough that no one could get through it. And over the years many young men tried. For it was rumoured that a beautiful girl lay sleeping behind it.

But, as the years went past, it seemed more and more like an old legend and no one remembered any of the people who lived in the palace. Then, one day, a king's son came riding by. He had heard the legend of the Sleeping Beauty and meant to

see if he could find her. He was very lucky, for the hundred years were nearly up and the hedge had lost its thorns. He pushed his way between the sweet-smelling roses and found himself in the courtyard where all the dogs lay asleep.

There was not a sound from the stables, except the gentle snoring of horses and up on the roof all the pigeons had their heads under their wings. The prince entered the hall and saw the king and queen, sleeping where they had collapsed on their thrones. In all the palace not a soul was awake.

The prince explored the whole palace and eventually

found the winding stair with the little room at the top. The bad fairy and the spinning-wheel had gone, but there on the bed lay the sleeping princess. The prince thought she was the most beautiful person he had ever seen. He couldn't resist; he just leaned over the bed and kissed her.

At that moment, the hundred years of the spell were over. The Sleeping Beauty woke up and smiled at the prince. He took her hand and led her downstairs to the hall, where her father and mother were waking up, too.

The fire started to burn in the kitchen grate, the meat began to roast again and there was soon food enough for a banquet. The prince and princess were married shortly afterwards and lived happily ever after.

Kate Crackernuts

Once there was a king and a queen who had each been married and each had a daughter. When they were unlucky enough to lose their wife and husband they each looked for someone else to marry. And as kings and queens don't have the same amount of choice as the rest of us, they picked each other.

They were married and were happy enough. The king's daughter was called Anne and the queen's was called Kate and the two girls became great friends. But the queen wasn't happy, because Anne was prettier than Kate.

So she plotted to see how she could take away Anne's good looks.

The queen went to see the hen-wife (who was also a witch) and told her the problem.

"Send the king's daughter to me tomorrow morning," said the old woman. "Only mind, she must have no breakfast before she comes."

"Anne, dear," said the queen sweetly, the next day. "Will you go to the hen-wife and see if she has any fresh eggs? Don't wait till after breakfast or all the best eggs will have been sold."

Anne obligingly skipped down to the village but, on the way, she picked up a crust from the freshly baked loaf cooling in the palace kitchen and munched it as she went.

When she reached the hen-wife's house, the old woman told her to lift the lid from a cauldron that was boiling on the fire and tell her what she saw there.

Anne thought this a strange place to look for eggs, but she did as she was told and saw nothing.

"Hm," said the hen-wife. "Haste ye back to the queen and tell her there are no eggs—and she should keep a lock on her pantry door!"

Anne didn't understand this either but she reported the message faithfully to the queen. Next morning, the queen sent Anne on the same errand, but this time she locked the kitchen door.

On the way to the village, Anne stopped to chat to some people who were harvesting peas. They gave her a handful of pods and she nibbled the sweet green young peas on her way to the hen-wife's cottage.

When Anne asked for the eggs, the same thing happened as the day before. The old woman told her to look in the pot and say what she saw, and Anne saw nothing. This time the message sent back was: "No eggs— and how do you expect the pot to boil when there's no fire?"

The queen understood the message a good deal better than poor Anne did and on the third morning she went with the girl to the hen-wife's house, making sure she ate nothing on the way.

This time, when Anne lifted the lid, her lovely head fell off and a sheep's head jumped out of the cauldron and settled on the girl's shoulders! Well, the queen had her wish now right enough, for her own daughter, Kate, was a good deal prettier than a sheep.

But Kate was furious when she heard what had happened. She took a fine silk scarf and wrapped it round her poor sister's head and both girls left the palace to seek their fortune.

They hadn't gone far when they

came to a fine castle. They knocked at the gate and were told that it belonged to a king who had two sons. One of the sons was very sick. He was tired out though he did nothing but lie in his bed all day. And the strange thing was that anyone who stayed up to watch the prince at night was never seen again, even though there was a fine reward of silver for anyone who could cure him.

"I'd like to try watching the prince," said Kate. "For my poor sister is sick, too, and I know what a sore trial it is."

So the king agreed to let the two girls stay, and that night Kate watched in the sick prince's bedroom. At midnight, the prince seemed to be sleeping, but he jumped out of bed and pulled on his boots and cloak and ran down the stairs to the stables. Kate ran lightly behind him and, when the prince whistled to his dog and saddled his horse, Kate jumped up behind him.

They rode out of the castle grounds and across country through the woods. And as they rode, Kate picked nuts off the trees and filled her apron with them. They came to a green hill with a door in it and the prince knocked.

"Who is it?" called a voice from inside.

"It is the prince, with his horse and his hound," said the young man.

"And his lady behind him," added Kate.

The door flew open and the prince rode in with his dog and Kate.

Inside was a magnificent fairy hall with feasting and dancing and music. Kate hid behind a pillar and watched while the prince danced and danced with the fairies till he was quite exhausted. Then they laid him down on a couch and fanned him till he was able to dance again.

When the cock crowed at daybreak, the prince left the fairy hall and rode back to the castle. In the morning, the king found the prince asleep in his bed and Kate sitting

by the fire, cracking nuts and eating them.

"He's had a good night, Your Majesty, but if you want me to watch another night, I'll need gold this time."

The king agreed and the next night everything happened as before. This time Kate saw a fairy baby playing with a wand in the corner. One of the older fairies said to another, "Just three taps of that wand and Kate's sister would be free of the sheep's head." Kate watched until no one was looking, then rolled some nuts towards the baby to play with. He dropped the wand and Kate immediately snatched it up.

At cockcrow, the prince rode back to the castle and Kate ran straight to Anne's room. She tapped her sister with the fairy wand and when Anne took the scarf off she had her own lovely face again. The sisters hugged and then Kate went back to the prince's room.

This time, when the king came in, Kate said she would stay up another night with the prince if she could marry him. The king agreed and on the third night everything happened as before. This time the baby was playing with a chicken and Kate heard a fairy say, "Three bites of that chicken would cure the prince." So she rolled some more nuts to the baby and was able to grab the chicken.

When the cock crowed, the prince rode back to the castle and Kate took the chicken to the kitchen. She plucked and roasted it and took it back to the prince's room. He woke to the smell of roast chicken and seemed to see Kate for the first time.

"That smells good," he said. "Can I have a bite?" When he had eaten the first bite, the prince sat up. Then he had another bite and jumped out of bed. After the third bite, he grabbed Kate round the waist and danced round the room with her. Then they sat down and cracked nuts together.

The king came rushing in when he heard the commotion and so did Anne and the other prince.

"The prince is cured," said Kate, blushing, "and I claim my reward."

"A sack of silver, a sack of gold and my son for a husband!" said the king. Then he saw his other son making eyes at Anne and knew that there would soon be another wedding.

So the two sisters married their princes and all four of them were as happy as larks.